This story was written with help from the clever
data scientists & engineers at GoDataDriven.

godatadriven.com

Mia got a puppy for her
birthday in May,
She named the dog Bowie
and taught him to stay.
He loved to stretch and
fetch and howl
And his favourite toy was
a purple, stuffed owl.

On a Tuesday they went
to a sunny dog park
Where she met Gravy, the dog,
and his owner, Mark.
Gravy was little, with big
eyes and a frown
And his favourite toy was a
fluffy pink crown.

Mia was so charmed by her new doggy friend
That she promised Gravy, they'd see him again.
So when they went home, she started a book
With his name, his address, and the toy that he took.

The next day she met Harry, Muppet, and Grace,
A trio of Labradors licking her face.
She ran home with Bowie to write down their names
And the toys that they love and their favourite games.

Weeks went by and Bowie grew
And they both met more dogs, so
her book grew too,
With daily notes about the latest
dog trends
And the games and the tricks Bowie
played with his friends.

Then on one rainy day
at her grandparents' place,
Her dog details book ran
out of space!
Mia was unsure what to do
'til she remembered the
person who she could turn to.

Mia ran to her Grams and
showed her the papers
That she'd written with Bowie
through all of their capers.
About big dogs and little, fluffy and sleek,
Where they lived, what they ate, and
what made them unique.

"So, what are your plans with this information?"
Asked Mia's Grams, with a slight hesitation.

Mia said... "I want to know if there's a pattern to find,
If dogs that love purple are also kind."

"Maybe big dogs live in this big part of town
And dogs that eat kibble are also brown.
Perhaps dogs whose names begin with a W
Are quiet and little and will not trouble you."

"All dogs are great, that's a fact to be said,
But which dogs will sleep at the foot of my bed?
Maybe dogs that nap could have owners who snore,
But it's too much to remember and I want to know
more."

Mia realised that her dog
details mission
Was just the start of a
greater ambition.
She wanted to know about all of the
dogs in the world,
But that's too much to
remember for one boy or one girl.

Her Grams listened close and
smiled ever so wide,
That her dentures nearly popped
out on one side.

She said, "wait here. I've got just
what you need!"
And fetched a computer to help
Mia succeed.

Computers are smart and they
do what they're told,
They're like Mia's dog book but
times one-thousandfold!
They hold more information than any one brain
Could keep and remember, deduce and maintain.

In her dog book, Mia had been writing down
Lots of data that she and Bowie had found.
And when her book finally ran out of space,
She built a computer database.

The computer could tell her what her data meant
And give her ideas for dog toys to invent.
It could tell her what were their favourite foods
And how the weather might change a poodle's
moods.

She could spend her
whole life typing up
Every fact about every
single pup,
Then with a couple of
clicks, and no wasted ink,
She'd have the answers to
questions before she
could blink.

FRANKIE!

Now, it's impossible to know
everything about every dog,
Even computers aren't up to the job.
But that didn't break Mia's resolve,
It's ok for some answers to be left
unsolved.

She'd have plenty of time to spend on this project,
There were more things to learn but there's no need to rush it.
Mia was happy that she now had the ability
To grow her data with this new utility!

But then ...

When she looked down at
Bowie, he was patiently
waiting
And Mia noticed the sweet
little face he was making.
His tail was wagging but if
dogs could talk,
He'd say, "Shut that thing
down, it's time for a walk!"

Thank you to GoDataDriven for being cool enough to let me write a children's book during company time.

Thank you to Edison who reassured me that just because this is a silly idea, that doesn't mean it isn't also a good one.

And thank you to Emily whose illustrations are so beautiful they made me cry.

- Camille

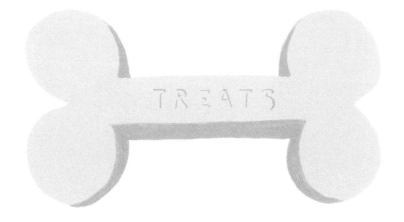

Made in the USA
Coppell, TX
12 September 2021